The Mystery Hidden in a Name

Written by
Kathleen Gorman

Illustrated by
Bonnie Lemaire

Halo
PUBLISHING
INTERNATIONAL

Heritage Fresno
2037 W. Bullard, Box 344
Fresno, CA 93711

ISBN: 978-1-63765-043-1
LCCN: 2021910426

Halo Publishing International, LLC
www.halopublishing.com

Printed and bound in the United States of America

I am grateful for the continued support and encouragement from my family. I want to thank my writing family, who continue to step up, listen, share and mentor. I am honored for the opportunity to create this story based on information shared by members of Heritage Fresno, and for their encouragement and wise advice. Heritage Fresno is a local nonprofit organization with the goal of enriching the future by preserving the past. A special thank you to Shannon at Wildflower Books for her help once again.

Weather today

4

"Today's lesson is all about names."

"What do you mean?" Merci asked her teacher.

"Do you know where your name came from? Were you named after a relative? Or does your name have a special meaning?" Ms. Fields asked.

She used her name as an example. "Many years ago, before my ancestors settled in America, their job was clearing fields after harvests in their homeland. They were known as men who cleared the fields. The name Fields stuck. Ever since it's been our family name."

George raised his hand. "I was named after my great uncle. He was in a war. He died at Pearl Harbor on a big ship."

"That is a special story. Now class, your project this week is to find out what you can about your names. You might find you have a special story too. Everyone will share on Friday."

The bell rang. "Time to go," Ms. Fields said. "Get your backpacks."

Merci couldn't wait to share with her parents. "Ms. Fields gave us our first assignment today," she announced at the dinner table. "It's all about our names."

"Names?" her dad asked.

"Who was I named after? Is there an ancestor named Merci?"

"No, but your name has a special story," her dad told her. "It goes back to World War I and World War II. Your great grandpapas fought in those wars."

"Like soldiers with guns and tanks and stuff?"

"During the First World War, there were no American tanks," her dad said. "Because they were foot soldiers, they traveled over 400 miles in boxcars. These boxcars transported forty soldiers or eight horses to the frontlines of the war zone."

"Boxcars that traveled on tracks like trains?"

"Yes. They were called Forty and Eight because of the cargo."

"Was the fighting hard?" asked Merci. "Why were they fighting? What's a frontline? Was the war zone where the fighting happened?"

"Both World Wars took place in France and other European countries," Merci's dad replied. "Your grandpapas were fighting for freedom. The fighting took place in the war zone, and the frontline was closest to the enemy."

"What does that have to do with my name?"

"The boxcars they rode in during the wars ended up being part of a huge humanitarian project after World War II," her dad said.

"What does that mean?" Merci asked.

"A project to help the French get back on their feet again," her dad explained. "The wars caused much damage, and the Americans wanted to do something. Farmers, businessmen, companies, and even families from across America filled boxcars with supplies."

"What did they put in them?"

"In Central California, farmers filled boxcars with dried figs and raisins," said her dad. "Other states added more equipment, clothing, food, and toys. Anything they thought the French could use to rebuild their country."

"The train traveled from the West Coast to the East Coast. Then the rail cars were loaded on freighters and shipped to France."

"Did you help too?"

He shook his head. "I wasn't born yet, but I've heard stories. The French were so touched by the generosity that they wanted to do something just as special for America."

"Dad, what about my name?"

"Let me get there," he told her. "The French searched their country for forty-nine of the original Forty and Eight boxcars. One for each state in the union at that time. They filled them with special items and shipped them to America. It was known as the Gratitude Train, translated to the Merci Boxcars."

"I am named after a boxcar. Now I get it."

"Not just a boxcar. Your great grandpapas were proud of the part they played, the freedom they fought for, and America's efforts to rebuild. When the Merci Boxcar arrived in Fresno, they were there to greet it."

"For many years, it stood in Roeding Park in central Fresno. Later, the city of Fresno moved it to the American Legion Fresno Federal Post 509, at 3509 N. First Street."

"You're right Dad, not just a boxcar," she smiled.

"Your greats wanted you to remember the gratitude expressed by the French. We honored their wishes when we named you Merci," Merci's dad said proudly.

"My name is special," Merci realized. "It brought countries together."

"You get it," said her dad.

"Merci means *thank you*!" Merci smiled. She felt proud of her name's special history.

Resources:

https://mgrsmembers.blogspot.com/2016/04/the-friendship-and-gratitude-trains.html

https://www.thefriendshiptrain1947.org

https://www.fortyandeight.org/history-of-the-408/

https://www.fresnobee.com/news/local/article220183440.html

http://www.themetrains.com/merci-train-boxcar-california.htm

https://www.amusingplanet.com/2016/05

CPSIA information can be obtained
at www.ICGtesting.com
Printed in the USA
BVHW021444270721
613003BV00021B/960

9 781637 650431